In loving memory of Hermia Soo —P.S.

To Hudson and Nolan, always and forever —M.P.D.

To my mom and grandma, the musical women in my life —Q.L.

GLOSSARY AND PRONUNCIATION GUIDE

There are tones used in Standard Mandarin Chinese that don't exist in English,
so the phonetic spellings below imitate the sounds as closely as possible.

húdié *(hoo-D'YEAH)*—butterfly

jiǎozi *(tzee'ow-ZA)*—dumplings

Nǎi Nai *(nigh NIGH)*—Grandmother

nǐ hǎo *(nee how)*—hello

Yé Yé *(yeah YEAH)*—Grandfather

Text copyright © 2024 by Phillipa Soo and Maris Pasquale Doran
Jacket art and interior illustrations copyright © 2024 by Qin Leng

Visit us on the Web! rhcbooks.com

Educators and librarians, for a variety of teaching tools, visit us at RHTeachersLibrarians.com

Library of Congress Cataloging-in-Publication Data is available upon request.
ISBN 978-0-593-56469-1 (trade) — ISBN 978-0-593-56470-7 (lib. bdg.) — ISBN 978-0-593-56471-4 (ebook)

The artist used ink, watercolor, and oil pastel to create the illustrations for this book.
The text of this book is set in 14.25-point Cotford Regular.
Interior design by Rachael Cole

MANUFACTURED IN CHINA
10 9 8 7 6 5 4 3 2 1
First Edition

PIPER CHEN
SINGS

written by **PHILLIPA SOO**

Grammy winner and Tony-nominated actress from *Hamilton*

and **MARIS PASQUALE DORAN**

illustrated by **QIN LENG**

RANDOM HOUSE STUDIO ▲ NEW YORK

T

his is Piper Chen.

Piper loves to sing.

She twirls through rooms . . .

bounces up the stairs,
and hops foot to foot,
always singing out a tune.

She sings good morning
to the peeking sun

and good night to
the cresting moon.

She sings to the orange-chested robins whistling outside her window and to the chanting frogs in the faraway pond, and they sing back to her.

Piper performs for
her closest friends,
with Spottie on backup.
Always.

She listens to Năi Nai's homemade jiăozi pop as they cook
and hums with pleasure as she eats them.

She hears the world's rich sounds as beats and rhythms
and adds her voice to its orchestra.

On a bright spring morning, Piper scoots to school, slapping her
foot against the pavement and bopping her head to the beat.

When Ms. Lopez takes attendance, Piper belts out,

"Here!"

She practices her whistle when she colors and cuts

and hums quietly while looking for the perfect book.

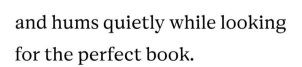

In her favorite class, Piper stands tall and is focused. She feels the chorus of voices vibrating through her.

When the class takes a break, Mr. Harris asks Piper if she wants to sing one of the solos in the Spring Sing. Piper lets her excitement answer,

"Yes!"

Yet when they start practicing again, something doesn't feel right. Piper is suddenly frozen, and she can only sing in a worried whisper.

"If you feel nervous, Piper, that is normal," Mr. Harris assures her. "You have the choice to sing a solo or sing with the class. Just tell me what you decide next time we meet."

When Piper returns home from school that day,

she does not twirl
through the rooms,

bounce up the stairs,
or hop foot to foot.

Piper is not singing.

Listening to the tune from Năi Nai's piano, Piper does not hum along. She does not sing one note.

Năi Nai is sitting upright at the piano bench, as she often does, one foot resting on the pedal, never wiggling or even rattling her teacup.

She starts playing their favorite song.

"Piper, I know you are there, but you aren't singing."

Piper climbs next to Năi Nai
and tells her about the solo.

"What if I forget the
words? What if I sound
like a frog?" she says.

"When we practiced,
I felt like butterflies were
having a dance party in
my belly! What if they
come back?"

Năi Nai pauses her playing
and smiles.

"Húdié," she says to Piper.
"What is húdié?" asks Piper.

"It is the Chinese word for butterfly,"
answers Năi Nai.

"I remember being your age, the very first time
I touched piano keys, playing along to the rain's
beat against the window."

Nǎi Nai plays the keys to sound like raindrops,
and Piper giggles.

"Before my first piano recital, the butterflies danced in me too.
'Go away, húdié!' I begged, but they just flew faster."

"They would only settle once I began to play."

"Eventually, I realized the butterflies visited to tell me when something exciting was ahead," Nǎi Nai explains.

"They flapped fast when I left China and traveled to America."

"And I felt them fluttering the day I graduated from music school."

"They flew through me
when I married your Yé Yé."

"They hovered over us when we brought
your father home for the first time."

"And they twirled unstoppably on
the day I became a U.S. citizen," she says.

"Now when they greet me, I greet them back.

'Hello, húdié. Nǐ hǎo.'"

"Piper, do you want to sing the solo?"

Piper blinks . . . and thinks . . . and nods.

Nǎi Nai resumes playing their favorite song,
and Piper finally sings along.

Weeks later, on the night of the show, Piper feels the butterflies flapping their wings and flying side to side.

When it is her class's turn to sing, they walk
out slowly. Piper sees the spotlight shining like
the bright, welcoming sun and its reflection
onstage like the inviting moon.

She hums to herself,

"Hello, húdié."

Piper steps into the glow, the butterflies
rest . . . and she sings.
  She sings like she sings to her stuffed
animals and Spottie the dog,
    the sun and moon and stars,
    the trees and birds and frogs.
  She sings because she loves to sing,
and her love is alive in that moment,
fluttering through her, her family and friends,
and her loving Năi Nai . . .

fluttering up and out into the world.